Even MONSTERS say GOOD NIGHT

By Doreen Mulryan Marts

Raintree is an imprint of Capstone Global Library
Limited, a company incorporated in England and
Wales having its registered office at 264 Banbury
Road, Oxford, OX2 7DY - Registered company
number: 6695582

www.raintree.co.uk
myorders@raintree.co.uk

Printed and bound in India

ISBN 978 1 4747 9044 4

British Library Cataloguing in Publication Data:
A full catalogue record for this book is available
from the British Library.

To my little girl, Avery, and your love of Halloween and questions.
Thank you for making the idea for this book possible!
– Mom

Avery never liked bedtime, and she liked it even less at Halloween when all the monsters were about.

Avery's mum tucked her into bed,
but Avery was NOT happy about it.
She knew there were monsters under her bed,
and probably in her wardrobe, too.

Her mum explained that monsters sleep in their OWN beds in their OWN homes. Then she turned off the light and shut the door.

Avery thought about this, but she wasn't so sure.
She had a few more questions for her mum.

"Ghosts sleep in big haunted houses."

"Yes. They must go to bed the moment their potions
are brewed for breakfast the next morning."

"They sleep in coffin beds inside pyramids."

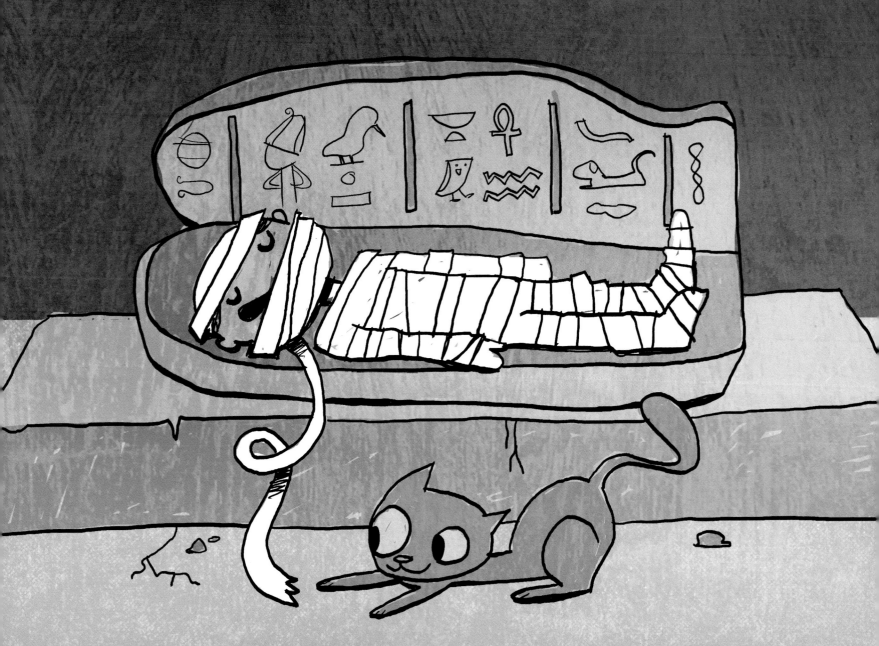

"Of course! They just sleep during the day instead of at night."

All the

Werewolves

Witches

Ghosts

Skeletons

Mummies

Vampires

are fast asleep, too.
Good night, my sweet girl.

So Avery went to bed,
but she still couldn't sleep.

She thought about all of the werewolves and witches
and ghosts and skeletons and mummies and vampires.

But Avery wasn't scared any more.